Poodle in a Pu

A story about a lost little doggy and the importance of microchipping your pet

Laura Fritz

Poodle in a Puddle: Published by Yawn's Publishing, 198 North Street, Canton, GA 30114, www.yawnspublishing.com

Visit Laura and Casey at: www.PoodleonaNoodle.com or contact them at: Casey@PoodleonaNoodle.com
Library of Congress Control Number: 2014942579 ISBN:978-1-940395-38-8
Printed in the United States of America

children

Little Casey woke up with the sun,
he stretched and he scratched
and he gave a big yawn.

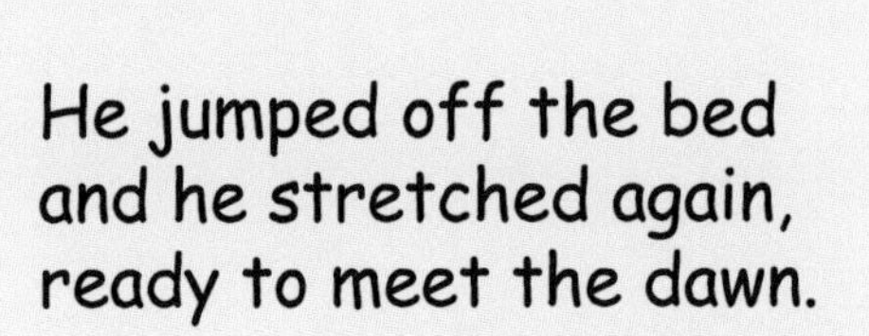

He jumped off the bed
and he stretched again,
ready to meet the dawn.

"Today is Saturday!" he exclaimed,
"Wakey, wakey, eggs and bakey day!
My family is home and I'm not alone,
on Saturday we play!

But first...we have pancakes!"

FAITH
5

Casey raced to the kitchen, but no one was cooking.
"No eggs? No bacon? No pancakes?
This can't be! It's Saturday, where is my family?"

He looked inside and outside,
he looked upstairs and down.
He looked here and there
and everywhere,
but his family was nowhere around!

7

His family goes fishing on Saturday
so Casey ran to the pond...
but there was no one on the dock.
He thought for sure they would be there
but sadly, no, they were not.

Suddenly he saw a rabbit
and rabbits are fun to chase,
so Casey ran after the rabbit
until the rabbit got away.

Casey chased the rabbit deep into the trees.
He got stuck in the bushes and brambles,
and he was covered with leaves.

CASEY JAMES

He struggled and tuggled and wiggled
until he finally broke free.

In all the huff his collar slipped off,
but Casey couldn't stop.

"I must be on my way!" he thought,
"I must find my family,
I must find them today!"

Casey's family likes to play ball
so he headed for the park.
He thought for sure they would be there
but sadly, no, they were not.

He'd only rest a minute,
and then be on his way.

"I must find my family!" he thought,
"I must find them today!"

Suddenly the sky turned dark
and it started to rain.
Poor little Casey was scared and cold and wet,
and he hadn't found his family yet.

A lady came by and what did she see?
"A Poodle in a puddle!
Oh my!
Poodles shouldn't be in puddles!
Poodles should be warm and dry!"

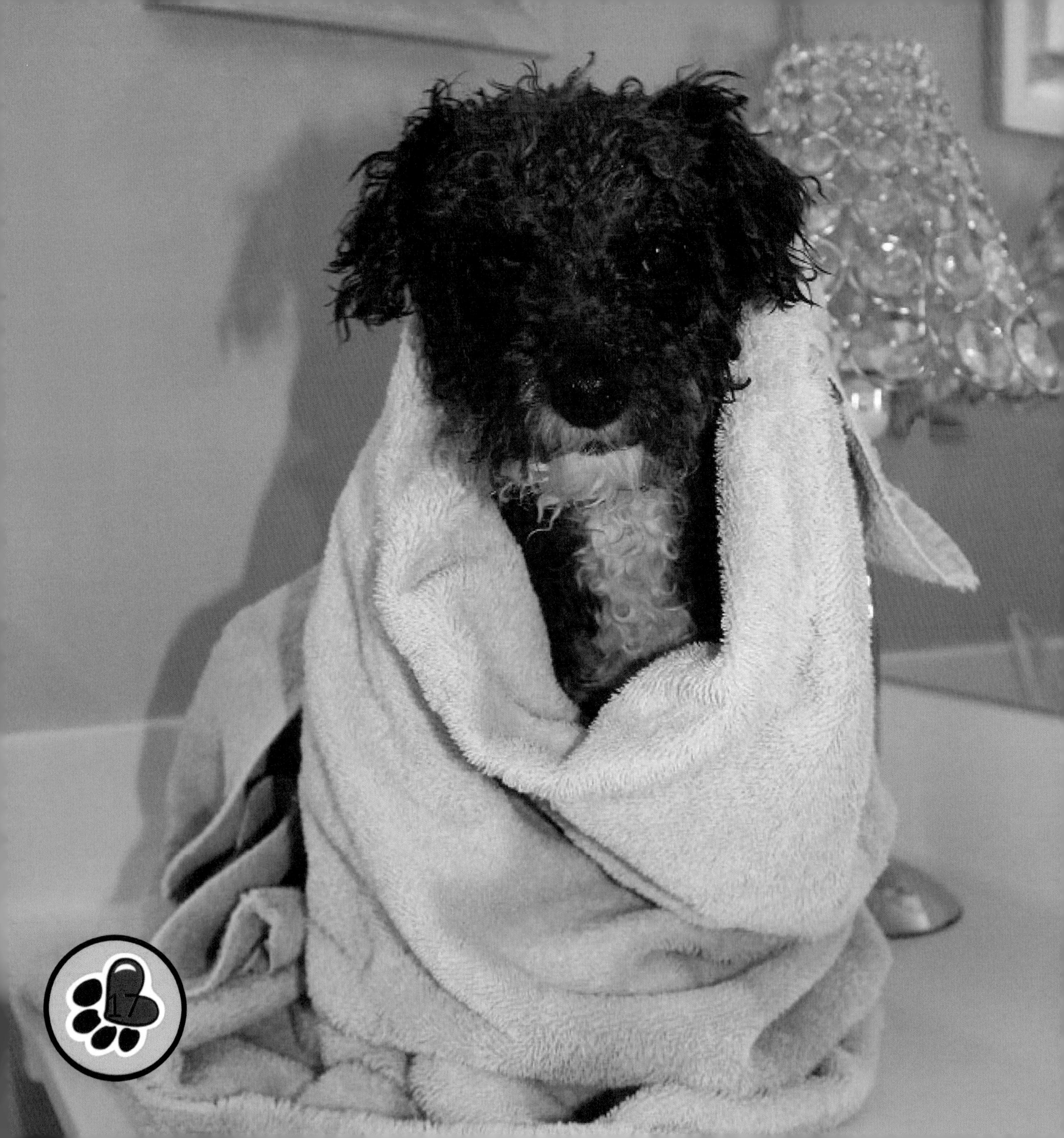

The lady scooped Casey up and gave him a hug.
"Come with me little guy," she said,
"I will make you warm and dry."

"Then I will take you to see Dr. Good,
he's a very good doctor you'll see.
Dr. Good will help us find your family!"

2013
iVet
Nutrition for
Why We Recommend iVet Pet Foods
Saturday

The lady explained that Dr. Good has many friends at Homeless Pets Foundation, and they find families for pets all across the nation.

"When a pet loses his family, Homeless Pets cares for him until his family comes back again.
And when a pet no longer has a home and is all alone, they find him a forever home!"

The lady took Casey to see Dr. Good
exactly like she said she would.

Phones were ringing
and dogs were barking
and people went in and out.

Dr. Good's office was very busy,
and little Casey was getting dizzy.

iVet
Nutrition for
MONDAY
TUESDA
Kennel Insurance

The girls in the office
gave him hugs and kisses
and little dog bones to chew.

They said, "Don't worry Casey,
Dr. Good will take good care of you!
You have a microchip, so we will find your
family lickety-split!"

Now, Casey didn't know it, but his family came back home.
Mama called for him, and Daddy called for him,
but Casey did not come.

Mama wasn't worried because she registered his microchip.
She knew if Casey ever got lost a vet could look it up,
and it wouldn't be long before she'd hold her little pup.

Mama and Daddy went to Casey's vet to see if anyone had found him.
But the vet said, "I'm sorry, Mrs. Fritz, but Casey isn't on our list.
When you microchip your pet, you must register the number.
Please check with the microchip company
to learn how to register your pet's ID."

"If you don't register the number, the microchip does no good.
I'm sorry we can't help you, but we really wish we could!"

His mama said, "Wait! I did register his number!
Please, please, look again and remember,
his name isn't Casey Fritz, his name is Casey James Parker."

The vet looked again and sure enough,
Casey James Parker's name came up!

A little while later, Casey and his family were finally back together.

"Today is Saturday, the day we play. Why did you leave me?" Casey cried.
His mama smiled and said, "Oh no son, today is Sunday.
We went to church today, and they don't let dogs in.
We were only gone a little while, and then we went back home again."

"We would never leave you! We love you, little Casey-Poo!"

About the Author and the Star of the Book:

Before Laura adopted Casey James Parker, he worked as a
show dog. His show name was Cash.
Laura enjoys photography, and at first Casey refused to have his
photo taken, turning his whole body away from Mama's camera.
Easily trainable and easy going, it didn't take long before he actually
began to pose!
Casey is a toy poodle; extremely smart, incredibly adorable,
sometimes demanding, and he will do just about anything
for chicken or cheese.

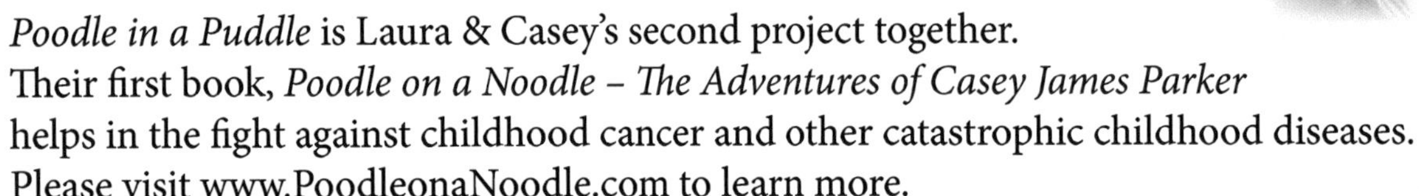

Poodle in a Puddle is Laura & Casey's second project together.
Their first book, *Poodle on a Noodle – The Adventures of Casey James Parker*
helps in the fight against childhood cancer and other catastrophic childhood diseases.
Please visit www.PoodleonaNoodle.com to learn more.

About Homeless Pets Foundation:

They come from a wide variety of backgrounds; students and teachers,
clubs and civic leaders, young and old, and they have one thing in
common; a commitment to saving the lives of homeless pets. They are
the Homeless Pets Foundation; dedicated to promoting responsible pet
ownership while placing adoptable dogs and cats in forever homes.

The **Homeless Pets Foundation**, founded in 1998 by Dr. Michael Good, consists of:
Homeless Pets Adoptions: Focusing on managing cats and dogs and their adoptions through Town and Country Veterinary Clinic in Marietta, GA.
Homeless Pet Clubs: Partnering with schools and workplaces, using their social networking abilities to help adopt out animals.
Homeless Pets Transport also known as the Underhound Railroad: Helping move shelter animals from the South to the North, where demand for these animals is higher, and loving families are waiting to adopt them.

Since its inception, Homeless Pets Foundation has placed over 10,000 animals in loving homes.
Please visit www.homelesspetsfoundation.com to learn more.

CPSIA information can be obtained
at www.ICGtesting.com
Printed in the USA
LVIC03n1159260914
405968LV00006B/36